Magic
Animal
Rescue

Maggie and the Wish Fish

Also by E. D. Baker

Magic
Animal
Rescue

Maggie and the Wish Fish

E. D. Baker

illustrated by
Lisa Manuzak

BLOOMSBURY
NEW YORK LONDON OXFORD NEW DELHI SYDNEY

First published in the United States of America in April 2017
by Bloomsbury Children's Books
www.bloomsbury.com

Bloomsbury is a registered trademark of Bloomsbury Publishing Plc

For information about permission to reproduce selections from this book,
write to Permissions, Bloomsbury Children's Books,
1385 Broadway, New York, New York 10018
Bloomsbury books may be purchased for business or promotional use. For
information on bulk purchases please contact Macmillan Corporate and
Premium Sales Department at specialmarkets@macmillan.com

Library of Congress Cataloging-in-Publication Data
Names: Baker, E. D., author. | Manuzak, Lisa, illustrator.
Title: Maggie and the wish fish / by E.D. Baker ; illustrated by Lisa Manuzak.
Description: New York : Bloomsbury, 2017. | Series: Magic animal rescue ; 2
Summary: Eight-year-old Maggie finds it harder each day to get along with
her stepmother and stepsiblings, but a talking fish promises to grant a
wish if she will free him.
Identifiers: LCCN 2016025137 (print) | LCCN 2016052967 (e-book)
ISBN 978-1-68119-143-0 (paperback) • ISBN 978-1-68119-313-7 (hardcover)
ISBN 978-1-68119-144-7 (e-book)
Subjects: | CYAC: Magic—Fiction. | Stepfamilies—Fiction. | Imaginary creatures—
Fiction. | Animals, Mythical—Fiction. | BISAC: JUVENILE FICTION /
Animals / General. | JUVENILE FICTION / Fairy Tales & Folklore /
General. | JUVENILE FICTION / Fantasy & Magic.
Classification: LCC PZ7.B17005 Mam 2017 (print) | LCC PZ7.B17005 (e-book)
|DDC [Fic]—dc23
LC record available at https://lccn.loc.gov/2016025137

Book design by Colleen Andrews
Typeset by Newgen Knowledge Works (P) Ltd., Chennai, India
Printed and bound in the U.S.A.
by Berryville Graphics Inc., Berryville, Virginia
2 4 6 8 10 9 7 5 3 1

This book is dedicated to my father, who taught me how to fish and gave me beautiful memories of drifting on a river with fishing poles in our hands. And to Quackers and Fromage, who taught me so much about eccentric wildfowl.

Magic
Animal
Rescue

Maggie and the Wish Fish

Chapter 1

Maggie's stepmother, Zelia, swished a long stick through the hot, soapy water. She scooped out a tunic and dropped it into another tub. Cool water splashed Maggie's face.

"That's the last of the laundry,"

said Zelia. "Rinse the rest of those things. I'm going inside to make lunch. After you've hung everything on the line to dry, you may come inside to eat. Be sure you don't drop anything. If you get something dirty, you'll have to wash it again."

Maggie nodded. "I'll be careful."

Once a week, she had to help with laundry. Her stepmother had lots of children to take care of, so there were always things to do.

Maggie had been busy ever since her father had gone to the far side of the forest to cut down trees a few weeks before. She wished she knew when he'd be back.

Maggie reached her hands into the tub of cool rinse water and pulled out one of the twins' shirts. After wringing out the water, she hung the little blue shirt on the line. As it dripped, the dirt below turned into mud.

Maggie was very careful not to

drop anything. She carried the clothes without letting them touch the ground. She hung them so they wouldn't slip off the rope. Her clothes got wet, but the laundry stayed clean. She always left her special journal of magical creatures somewhere safe on laundry day.

When lunch was ready, Zelia called all the other children inside. Maggie wasn't finished with the laundry so she tried to work faster. All that work made her extra hungry.

Maggie was hanging the last tunic when she heard a sudden whoosh of wings. Five flying pigs soared over the treetops. They landed in the mud under the dripping laundry. *Oh no!* Maggie thought. The pigs splashed and played in the mud. "Go away!" she shouted. "Stop that!" The pigs splattered big globs of mud all over the laundry. Maggie would have to wash everything again!

She tried to chase the pigs away, but they flew into the air. Chasing each other between the hanging laundry, the pigs splashed even more mud on the clothes.

Maggie wasn't sure what to do. Part of her loved watching the pigs fly, but they were going to get her in real trouble. She tugged on her special unicorn tip. If only it worked on pesky flying pigs!

"Get out of here!" she shouted. When that didn't work, she threw rocks at the pigs to scare them. The pigs finally flew away.

Just then, Zelia came outside and saw Maggie throwing rocks. She did not see the flying pigs. "What are you doing?" she demanded. "What did you do to the laundry?"

"I was chasing off some flying pigs," said Maggie. "They got the laundry muddy!"

"Flying pigs? Ha!" said Zelia. "Maggie, your lies are getting

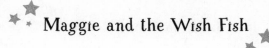

bigger every day. There is no such thing as a flying pig!"

"But the pigs *were* here!" cried Maggie. "They flew away right before you came outside."

"I saw you throwing rocks at our clean clothes, but I didn't see any pigs!" said her stepmother. "Now you have to wash everything again yourself."

Maggie sighed. "I know," she said. She knew she shouldn't argue. She'd only get in more trouble if she did. Zelia stomped back inside as Maggie took all the clothes off the line again and put everything back into the soapy water. She scrubbed and scrubbed until her hands were sore. When each item was clean, Maggie dropped it into the tub of cool water. She rinsed and rinsed, then hung the clothes on the line.

Maggie was finally about to go inside for lunch when she heard the *whoosh* of wings again. The pigs were coming back! Maggie grabbed a stick and waved it in the air as the pigs circled around the laundry. "Go away!" Maggie shouted until her throat was sore and the pigs finally flew off.

Zelia came outside again. "Why were you shouting *this* time?" her stepmother asked.

"The pigs came back," said Maggie.

"Stop lying!" Zelia told her. "You can have something to eat when you learn to tell the truth."

Chapter 2

The next day, Maggie woke before the sun came up. Zelia had taken away her bed a few days before. Her stepbrother Peter slept on it now. Maggie slept in the loft with some of the other children. She shared a mattress with her stepsister, Jenny, and the twins, Timmy and Tommy. When Maggie sat up, the straw-stuffed mattress crinkled. One of the twins muttered and rolled over. Maggie slid off the bed as quietly as she could. She held her breath as she climbed down the ladder. Tiptoeing out of the cottage, she shut the door behind her.

If she'd waited any longer, Zelia would have woken up and found something for her to do. But

Maggie couldn't stay at home today. She needed to go see Bob, the stableman in charge of magical animals. He would know what to do about those flying pigs.

Maggie started down the path as the sun was coming up. She spotted a doe leading her fawn, and a heron wading in a pond.

Maggie turned onto the road leading to the castle. She passed a gnome tending his mushroom garden. "Hello!" she called.

"Hello, yourself," he replied.

Maggie glimpsed fairies sipping dew from flowers. "Good morning!" she said, waving. The fairies giggled and waved back.

Out of nowhere, she saw someone—or some*thing*—coming toward her.

Maggie remembered the troll that had once chased her. She darted from the road and hid behind a thick tree trunk. A mother manticore strolled past with her three cubs trailing behind her. When the manticores were out of sight, Maggie returned to the road. She looked both ways, but no one was coming.

Maggie passed the old ruins and then the mill. Finally, she passed the castle and saw Bob's cottage.

Bob was in the stable, feeding the animals their breakfast.

"Look who's here!" said Leonard, the talking horse. "You're up early. I haven't even had my grain yet."

"Hi, Leonard! Hi, Bob! I'm sorry to interrupt, but I need to talk to you, Bob," said Maggie.

"Is everything all right?" Bob asked her.

"Not really. I'm having trouble with flying pigs," Maggie said.

Bob nodded. "I've had a lot of

trouble with flying pigs myself. Here," he said, handing her his journal. "You should find what you need to know in this."

"What about my grain?" asked Leonard. "I'm starving! Why am I always the last one to get breakfast?"

Maggie giggled. Leonard was as fat as a tick and looked like he'd never missed a meal.

Bob sighed. "The last to eat and the first to complain. You know, I've been thinking about putting you on a diet."

"Never mind," said Leonard. "There's no need to get nasty!"

Chapter 3

While Bob finished feeding the magical animals, Maggie sat on an overturned bucket and looked through the journal. Leonard munched his grain, twitching his ears each time she turned a page.

Flying Pigs

Most common wing colors: white, gray, pale blue, speckled black, spotted pink

Behavior: often travel in clusters of at least three pigs. Rarely seen at night. Believed to nest high up in tall trees. Rarely observed sleeping.

Bad habits: eating plants they shouldn't, rooting up gardens, smearing mud on things. This is particularly troublesome when they appear in large groups.

Habitats: muddy riverbanks; muddy fields after a heavy rain; mud anywhere; cornfields; apple orchards; barley, alfalfa, or clover fields; around beehives; well-shaded forests

Ailments: prone to sunburn and skin conditions such as excessive dryness and rashes. Often get hoof rot from wet mud. Wallowing in mud may cause damage to wing feathers.

Favorite foods: corn, apples, barley, alfalfa, clover, stolen fruit pies

What to do to prevent flying pig infestation: flying pigs do not like shifting light patterns or bright, contrasting colors. To shoo them away, flap a brightly colored cloth in the air. To keep them away, hang strips of brightly colored fabric from a line strung between two poles.

Beware of flying pigs that appear to be thinking. They are smarter than they look.

Bob came back just as Maggie finished reading the journal entry. "Thank you for showing this to me," she said, handing the journal to him. "I think I know what to do now."

Chapter 4

Leonard and Bob gave Maggie a ride home. Maggie told them about seeing the manticores, but they didn't see any new magical creatures.

"You can drop me off here," Maggie said when she spotted the path leading to her cottage. "I don't want you to waste any more time!"

"Are you sure?" asked Bob. "It isn't that much farther to your cottage."

"I'm sure," said Maggie as she slipped off Leonard's back. "I'll be fine."

"See you around, short stuff," said Leonard, and started off at a trot.

Maggie hurried down the path toward home. Her stomach grumbled, reminding her that she was

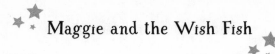

very hungry. When she came across wild raspberry bushes, she stopped to pick some and filled her basket with berries.

After eating her fill and picking enough for everyone in the family, she started walking again. It was still early morning.

Maybe her stepmother wouldn't be too mad that she'd left without asking. Maybe she hadn't even noticed that Maggie was gone!

When Maggie reached the cottage, Zelia was taking fresh bread out of the oven. "Where have you been?" she asked when Maggie stepped inside.

"I was out picking raspberries for everyone," said Maggie. She dumped the berries into a bowl. When her stepmother wasn't looking, Maggie borrowed her bright red shawl. Maggie couldn't wait to try out the tips about chasing away flying pigs that she'd learned from Bob's journal. She also wanted to prove to Zelia that she wasn't lying.

Maggie went behind the cottage to the spot where she and Zelia usually did the laundry. Hoping to attract the pigs, she poured water on the dirt, turning it into mud. When Maggie heard the whoosh of

wings, she grabbed the red shawl and flapped it at the flying pigs.

"Stepmother, come here!" she cried. "The flying pigs are back. I want you to see them."

Zelia walked outside, but the flying pigs were already gone.

"This nonsense again? And what are you doing with my shawl, young lady?" cried Zelia.

"I borrowed it to chase away the flying pigs," Maggie told her.

"There are no flying pigs!"

shouted Zelia. "And borrowing without asking is stealing, which makes you a liar and a thief. No supper for you tonight, Maggie!"

"But I wasn't stealing! I didn't lie!" Maggie cried. "Why won't you listen to me?"

"I don't listen to liars!" Zelia said and stormed off.

Maggie's throat felt tight as she held back tears. She'd never felt so alone before.

Chapter 5

The next day, a storm passed through, bringing wind and pounding rain. Peter didn't take his sheep out that morning because of it. After the storm passed and the sun came out, he dug worms out of the mud and announced that he was going fishing.

His mother handed him a big basket. "Take Maggie with you. She can help carry the fish home. Here, Maggie," she said, handing her a smaller basket. "You can pick more berries while Peter is fishing."

Maggie took the basket and followed Peter out the door. They hadn't gone far when he handed her the big basket. "Here, you can carry this one, too," he said.

Maggie sighed. She was tired of doing Peter's work for him.

As they walked, Peter swung the long stick he used for fishing. He whacked flowers blooming on the side of the path. He knocked leaves from trees. He even tried to hit a passing sparrow. Afraid that he might whack her next, Maggie dropped back to follow him from a safe distance.

After they reached the lake, Peter walked down to the shore

and cast his line while Maggie started looking for berries.

"You won't believe how many fish I'm going to catch!" Peter announced. He pulled in his line, but the worm was gone. He put on another one and cast again. Maggie stumbled upon a lush blackberry thicket and began to fill her basket. She popped one into her mouth and bit down. The taste was refreshing but the seeds got stuck between her teeth.

An hour later, Peter had caught only two tiny fish. Meanwhile, Maggie's basket was almost filled to the top with delicious, ripe berries.

Peter started casting and pulling his line in faster. He used up almost *all* of his worms . . . and yet he didn't catch any more fish.

Maggie thought he looked angry, so she moved farther down the berry patch and closer to the lake.

A fish jumped in the lake near Maggie and left a big circle in the water.

"Why don't you try over here?" she called to Peter. "I just saw a really big fish!"

Peter laughed. "Yeah, right. You don't know anything about fishing!"

He cast his line once more, but it came back without a fish again. Peter was scowling when he stomped over to Maggie's spot. He cast his line where she had been standing and felt a tug right away.

"Look at this!" Peter shouted as he pulled in a very big fish. He smiled and glanced at Maggie. "I knew this was a good spot!"

Maggie squeezed her lips shut so she wouldn't say anything. Not a lot surprised her anymore. She was used to Peter taking the credit for the good things and blaming her for the bad.

The fish wiggled and thrashed

on his line. Peter unhooked it and handed it to Maggie. "Put it in the basket, then come back for the next one. I'm going to catch lots of big ones now."

The fish stopped squirming as soon as Maggie held it. She was carrying the fish to the basket when it suddenly said, "Let me go and I'll grant you a wish."

Maggie's eyes grew large and her mouth dropped open. "You can talk!" she said.

"It's not as unusual as people think," said the fish. "Let me go and I'll grant you a wish."

"What kind of wish?" Maggie asked.

"Whatever you want," said the fish. "But first you have to let me go."

Maggie thought of all the things she could wish for. Getting her old bed back would be nice. So would having enough to eat. But belonging to a nicer family would be wonderful! Yes, that's what she wanted more than anything. Besides, should they really eat a talking fish?

Maggie carried the fish to the lake. "Shouldn't I tell you my wish now before you swim away?" she asked.

"I need to get back in the water!" the fish said, gasping. "Hurry! I can't breathe!"

Maggie quickly let the fish slip back into the water and watched as it disappeared into the murky depths.

"Wait, don't you want to know about my wish?" she called after it. But the fish didn't come back.

"I wish to be part of a nicer

family!" she said in a quiet voice so Peter wouldn't hear her.

There was no sign of the fish, not even a ripple in the water where he'd been. Maggie was sure she'd been fooled.

Peter was whistling when he rejoined Maggie. "We need to go home now. It looks like it's going to rain. I don't think I'll catch any more fish anyway. But at least I caught that big one. It should feed everyone tonight. Mother will be

45

so proud of me! Hey, where is it?" he asked, looking into the basket.

"Um, I let it go," said Maggie. "It was a talking fish."

"You what?" shouted Peter.

"It said it would grant me a wish if I let it go. I was going to wish for something for the family."

"That was our supper! Fish don't talk! I'm telling Mother what you did." Peter snatched the big basket from her hand and stomped off toward home without Maggie.

Maggie sighed. "I'm sure you will," she said to herself, thinking about how she wouldn't get any supper again. She was so tired of falling asleep hungry when she was just trying to do the right thing!

Chapter 6

Maggie couldn't blame Peter for being angry. She was angry, too! The fish had lied and tricked her into letting it go. Zelia would have been so happy if she had seen that fish! Now they didn't have supper and Maggie didn't have a wish because she had actually believed a talking fish.

Maggie started to walk home alone, dragging her feet all the way. She knew how angry her stepmother would be when she got there. Knowing that she probably wouldn't get supper again, Maggie nibbled a handful of the berries she had collected.

She hadn't gone far when she heard a girl crying. Maggie hurried down the path, where she found a girl with dark brown braids clutching a long, pink ribbon. When the girl saw Maggie, she used her fists to scrub tears from her eyes.

"What's wrong?" Maggie asked.

"My goose got away," said the girl. "I don't know how to find her."

"I can help you look for her," said Maggie. "What's your goose's name?"

"Eglantine," the girl told her. "My name is Stella. My father told me to watch her today. She's a very special goose. If you see her, you'll know it's Eglantine. She's much prettier than most geese and her feathers are beautiful snowy white."

"That's a lovely name," said Maggie. "If we both look, we should be able to find her."

"We need to hurry. Father expects me back before it starts to rain again," Stella said.

Searching the nearby shrubs, Maggie called out for the goose. "Eglantine! Eglantine!"

Stella called out, too, looking in the tree branches above.

They each took one side of the path. The girls looked and looked, but there was no sign of Eglantine.

"What does she like to eat?" asked Maggie.

"She likes corn and oats and cracked wheat," said Stella. "And also mosquitoes and flies and tadpoles."

"I know where we might find some tadpoles," said Maggie. She led the girl back down the path to the lake. They walked around the lake to the shallow end. There they saw a goose with sparkling white feathers chasing tadpoles.

"Eglantine!" cried Stella.

The goose snatched a tadpole out of the water.

"Does she usually come when you call her?" asked Maggie.

"Only at feeding time," said Stella.

"Do you have any feed for her?"

"Not with me."

"I have an idea," said Maggie. She stepped into the water and tried to catch some tadpoles, but they were too fast and slippery. After slipping and sliding and nearly falling down, she decided that she wasn't going to be able to catch them with her hands. Taking off her shoe, she used it to scoop up water.

"Aha, gotcha!" Maggie smiled. She had caught two tadpoles. Moments after she'd set the tadpoles on the ground, the goose waddled out of the water and devoured them.

"Eglantine!" Stella cried, throwing her arms around the goose. She slipped the ribbon around the goose's neck.

Suddenly, the goose sat down. When she stood up, a golden egg lay on the ground.

"Here, this is for you," Stella

said. She handed the golden egg to Maggie.

Maggie gasped. "Are you sure?" she asked. "This looks like gold!"

"Oh yes. I'm sure," said Stella. "Eglantine lays them all the time. Thank you for helping me find her!"

Maggie examined the egg. It looked like real gold to her!

When Stepmother sees this, maybe she won't be so mad after all! she thought.

Chapter 7

Dark clouds were rolling in when Maggie finally reached the cottage. Her heart sank when she saw Zelia and Peter waiting for her on the front doorstep.

"What were you thinking?" Zelia

snapped. "Peter said you let a fish go—on *purpose*!"

Maggie nodded. "It's true, I did. But it was a talking fish. It promised to grant me a wish if I let it go."

"Fish don't talk, Maggie. You probably just heard its last gasps of air. You always let your imagination run wild! This time you cost the entire family a nice supper!" Zelia shouted.

"I brought berries with me, though," said Maggie.

"Berries and two little fish. That's not enough for supper! You don't think of anyone but yourself. And what took you so long to get back here?"

"I was right behind Peter, but then I helped a girl catch her goose. I brought you this, Stepmother." Maggie held out the egg.

"What is that?" asked Peter, taking it from her.

"A golden egg," said Maggie. "Be careful with it! The goose laid it. The girl gave it to me for helping her."

61

"That's ridiculous!" exclaimed Zelia. "There is no such thing as a goose that lays golden eggs."

"Wait, Mother. Look at this," Peter said. He handed the egg to her. "I think it might be real."

Zelia looked exasperated. She held the egg as if she was going to throw it away . . . until she examined it more closely. She rubbed it with her finger, gently digging her fingernail into it. "It just might be," Zelia said under her breath.

She turned back to Maggie. "Where did you say you got this?"

"The girl who owned the goose gave it to me," said Maggie.

Zelia's eyes narrowed. "The girl has a goose that lays golden eggs and all you got was one egg? Why didn't you bring home the goose? Do you know how much we could have used all of its eggs?"

"It wasn't mine to bring

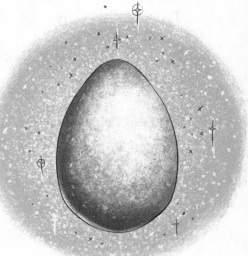

home," Maggie replied. "Eglantine belongs to another family."

Zelia's face turned red. "You lose our supper and a golden goose all in one day! I can't believe it. I'm sick and tired of your foolishness and all your lies. You cost us more than you're worth. I don't want you here any longer."

Tears began to fill Maggie's eyes. "What are you saying?"

"You're no longer welcome in this cottage. Go away, Maggie, and don't ever come back!"

"I was born in this cottage! I've lived here my whole life," Maggie cried. "This is my home! Father would never make me leave home like this!"

"But he's not here, so I'm in charge. This isn't your home anymore," said Zelia. "It's time for you to find a new one!"

Maggie scrubbed the tears from her eyes with her knuckles. She didn't like Zelia and Peter anyway. Any place would be better without them!

Chapter 8

It started to rain as Maggie walked away from the cottage. Angry and bewildered, her tears felt hot on her cheeks. How could Zelia kick her out? If only Maggie could tell her father!

Maggie stumbled down the path as the rain poured and the wind blew. She wasn't thinking about where she was going.

The wind got colder. Maggie shivered and looked around. She had reached the main road. In a few hours, it would be night. Then she wouldn't be able to find her way.

Maggie wondered what she should do. She didn't have any relatives around who could take her in. Bob was the only person who had been really nice to her, but his magic stable was so far away. She would be soaked to the bone before she made it that far!

Thunder rumbled as she stopped to think. She needed to find a place where she could get out of the storm. Although she knew of a few caves where she would be dry, none of them were empty. A grumpy black bear lived in one. A family of wolves lived in another. Something she'd never seen lived in the third, but she had heard it growl and she definitely didn't want to go any closer. Maggie saw that she wasn't far from the ruins. She hurried along the path. Her wet clothes clung to her body, making her more uncomfortable. Water streamed from her hair. When she finally spotted the ruins, she climbed over the first big rocks and crawled under the next big ones. Finding a dry spot big enough for her, she sat down, shivering.

A rock fell. Suddenly, other rocks scraped against each other.

"Owiee! I stub my big toe! It hurt," a voice cried out.

"You have big feet!" said another voice. "You always stub toe."

Maggie huddled in her space between the rocks. She had heard

these voices before: once in a field of wild flowers, and once on the road with Bob and Leonard. The goblins were here and they sounded close by.

Maggie dug around in her pocket until she found a small, hard triangle. It was the tip of the silver unicorn's horn that he had given to her when she pulled prickers from his mane. The little piece of horn was the only thing that could protect her now. Bob had told her that unicorn horns destroyed poison. There was poison in goblin blood. Any goblin that even touched a unicorn horn would go *poof!* and vanish. Maggie took the tiny piece out of her pocket and held it tightly in her hand.

Thunder boomed overhead. "Agh!" shrieked the goblins.

"Me hate thunder!" cried one.

"Me hate it more!" yelled another.

"Me hate it most!" shouted the third. "Quick, under rock before thunder get us."

Maggie waited, her heart pounding as the goblins came closer. The moment they stuck their heads under her big rock, Maggie held up the piece of unicorn horn. The piece of horn began to glow. The goblins screamed.

"Unicorn!" they cried. Their faces disappeared from the opening.

The goblins were clumsy as they ran away and bumped into everything. Small rocks bounced against bigger rocks while other rocks crashed to the ground. Maggie

73

waited until she couldn't hear them anymore before she crawled out from under the rocks. She peeked her head out and made sure everything was clear before setting out again. When she safely reached the path, she started to run. The goblins were gone, but other creatures would be looking for shelter. There was only one place where she was sure she'd be safe even though it wouldn't be easy to get to—the magic stable.

Maggie slipped and slid as she

ran down the road. Tripping over a rock, she landed on her hands and knees in a puddle.

"Ow!" Maggie cried. She was just getting to her feet when she felt something nudge her from behind. Startled, she turned around and found the silver unicorn that had once chased away the goblins. It was the same unicorn that had given her the tip of his horn. She gasped when the unicorn knelt down, as if offering her a ride.

When the unicorn didn't move,

Maggie climbed onto his back. She dug her fingers into his mane and held on as he started to gallop down the road. Pounding rain stung her eyes, and cold wind chilled her as the unicorn carried her past the mill, beyond the castle, and all the way to Bob's stable.

It was pitch dark when Maggie slipped off the unicorn's back. "Thank you!" she told him, stroking his cheek. "You saved me twice now!"

The unicorn nickered, bumping her with his head. When he turned and disappeared into the storm, Maggie hurried into the stable, dripping wet from head to toe. She found an empty stall where she piled clean hay in a corner and curled up, still shivering.

The stable was warm and soon she was sound asleep.

Chapter 9

"She must have showed up during the storm last night."

Maggie woke and rubbed her eyes. At first she didn't know where she was. She didn't remember until she heard Leonard's voice as he

79

continued speaking. "She's in the stall next to Patrick and Marsden."

Maggie sat up. She was pulling hay from her hair when Bob peeked in the stall. "Good morning, Maggie. You spent the night here?" he asked.

Maggie nodded. "I'm sorry. I promise I didn't touch or hurt anything. And I tried not to use much hay."

"I'm not worried about that!" said Bob. "Just tell me what happened. Why are you here?"

As she told Bob about everything that her stepmother had said, Maggie's eyes filled with tears again. She didn't want to cry in front of him, but she couldn't seem to help it. She felt so alone and missed her father terribly.

"Your stepmother kicked you out of your home during the storm last night?" said Bob. "That weather wasn't fit for anyone— human or beast!"

Maggie nodded again.

"I can't believe you walked all that way in this terrible weather!" said Bob.

"I walked only part of the way," Maggie told him. "I hid in the ruins for a while, but I left after the goblins found me. I scared them off with my own piece of unicorn horn. You won't believe it, but the silver unicorn came along and gave me a ride here!"

"Goblins! I'm glad you had that piece of horn with you. And to think the unicorn came by just then! It sounds as if you've made a good friend," Bob said.

"Do you really think so?" Maggie asked, her eyes shining through her tears. "When he first showed up, I couldn't believe that a unicorn had come to help me."

"Unicorns don't help just anyone," said Bob. "He must think you're very special. Don't you worry, Maggie. You're welcome to stay here for as long as you want!"

"Thank you!" Maggie told him. She coughed. A moment later, she coughed again.

"Are you all right?" asked Bob. He knelt down to feel her fore-head. "You have a fever! No wonder, being out in a storm like that. I'll be right back. Stay here while I get something for your fever."

Maggie lay down again. She wasn't feeling very well. Then Maggie realized that she must have dozed off, because a few minutes later she opened her eyes and Bob was back.

"Drink this. It's my own recipe," he said, spooning medicine into her mouth. He handed her a cup of hot tea.

Maggie drank the tea, listening to Bob go from stall to stall as he fed the magical animals. She wanted to help, but she didn't have the strength to get up and offer. Instead, she fell asleep again. While she slept, she dreamed of flying pigs. They smeared mud all over row after row of clean laundry hanging on clotheslines. When Zelia appeared in the dream, the pigs smeared mud all over her, too.

Maggie woke as Bob came back with a bowl of chicken soup. She was eating the soup when an older woman entered the stall. The woman took one look at Maggie and said, "This won't do at all!"

"I'm sorry," Maggie said as she started to get up. "I didn't mean to trouble anyone. I'll leave now."

"You most certainly will not!" said the woman. "I'm Nora, Bob's wife. He told me what happened. Sending a young girl like you out into a storm! It's disgraceful! And now you're sick. Listen, we have an extra bed in our cottage and you're welcome to it. I just got everything ready for you. Come inside right now, young lady. We'll get you better in no time!"

Chapter 10

Maggie lay back in the bed and sighed. It wasn't at all like the bed her father had made, with its lumpy straw mattress that poked her. This one had a feather mattress and soft, warm blankets. It was so comfortable that she wasn't sure she'd ever want to get up.

Maggie had been in the cottage for two days and slept most of the time. She'd taken a lot of Bob's medicine and eaten a lot of Nora's chicken soup. She was finally starting to feel better, but her dreams had been filled with flying pigs, talking fish, a silver unicorn, and a scolding stepmother.

"Nora says you can probably get up tomorrow," said Bob. "But you should still rest today. I thought you might like something to read in the meantime." He handed her his journal.

"Thank you!" said Maggie. "There are a couple animals I'm curious about, and I want to look them up."

As soon as Bob left, Maggie turned to the entry about talking fish. The entry wasn't very long.

"I wish I'd read this earlier," said Maggie. She turned the page until she found the entry about geese.

Talking Fish

There are many sorts of talking fish. Although they may vary in size and type, they all have one thing in common: they all promise to grant wishes if you let them go. Only a few will keep their promises. Even then they do it in unexpected ways. Because so many of them are lying, it is better not to trust a talking fish. More often than not, the larger the fish, the bigger the liar.

Geese That Lay Golden Eggs

Such geese are very rare and valuable.
Whoever has one should not let anyone
know. Most owners of these geese end up
melting down the golden eggs. This way,
merchants and tax
collectors do not
know that the gold
came from a goose.
Thieves consider
these geese a real
prize. However, the geese lay golden eggs
only for people who love them and take
good care of them. Anyone else will get
ordinary eggs.

Food: the same as for any goose. Corn, cracked wheat, and barley are the most common types of feed.

Housing: Most owners keep their geese inside their homes at night. However, the geese need plenty of fresh air and sunshine as well as clean water for drinking and swimming.

"I am so glad I didn't take that goose to Zelia," Maggie said as she closed the journal. "It definitely would have laid ordinary eggs for her. She probably would have cooked it!"

Chapter 11

Maggie felt fine the next day. She got out of bed when she heard Nora and Bob talking. After getting dressed, she left the tiny bedroom where she'd slept and found Bob putting on his shoes. Nora was pouring three cups of hot tea.

"Good morning!" Nora said when she saw Maggie. "How do you feel?"

"Great!" said Maggie. "Thank you for everything you've done. I think it's time for me to go. You've been really nice and I don't want to bother you anymore."

"You said that your father is away, but do you have any other relatives you can trust?" asked Bob. "Is there anywhere else you can stay?"

Maggie shook her head. "My

grandmother died a few years ago. I don't have any other relatives or anyplace else to go."

"Then you're staying here with us, at least until your father comes back!" said Nora. "I won't hear of you leaving."

"Are you sure you don't mind?" Maggie said.

"Of course, I'm sure! We love having you here," Nora told her. "Our daughter moved out years ago. She has her own family now

and lives far away. Our house is too empty!"

"And I could use your help," said Bob. "I'm getting too old to do the things I used to do. One of the flying pigs in the barn had piglets last night. They'll be ready to learn how to fly in a few weeks. I'll need help teaching them, and keeping them from getting into trouble once they can fly. I'll let them go in the forest when they're old enough, but that will be months from now. They're very cute when they're piglets. And I know some tiny horses who would love to have someone feed them raspberries."

"Could I really help you?" Maggie asked. "I'd like that more than anything! Teaching a piglet how to fly sounds like so much fun!"

"Then it's settled!" said Nora. "You're staying here with us! Now, before you go out to feed the animals, you both need to eat a good breakfast. Have a seat at the table while I start the eggs."

"I'd rather help you if I could," said Maggie. "I like to cook."

Nora smiled. "That would be wonderful! It's been so long since we had extra help around—"

Bang! Bang! Bang! Someone was knocking on the door. Bob and Nora exchanged a look. Bob stood up and went to answer it.

Maggie was surprised to see Peter and Zelia standing outside.

"We finally found you!" said Zelia. "Peter has spent days looking for you. He had to ask all over to find this place. It's time to go, Maggie."

"What's this?" said Bob. "I thought you kicked her out of your cottage."

Zelia shrugged. "I made a mistake. I want her back now."

"I'm not going back!" said Maggie. "I'm staying here with Bob and Nora."

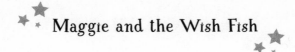
"Don't be foolish," Zelia said, and waved Peter into the cottage.

Peter grabbed Maggie's arm and pulled her toward the door. "You're coming home with us."

"Let go of me!" Maggie cried. "I'm not going anywhere with you!"

"Let her go, boy!" Bob ordered, blocking the way to the door. "Maggie lives here now."

Peter dropped Maggie's arm.

"I'm her stepmother!" cried Zelia. "She has to do what I say. You two have no right to stand in my way."

"You said I couldn't live with you anymore," cried Maggie. "Those were your words, and I don't care if you changed your mind. I'm not living with you again."

"You ungrateful girl!" shouted Zelia. "After all I did for you despite your lies and laziness."

"It's time you said good-bye," Bob said. He hustled Peter and Zelia to the door.

Bob was about to close the door when Zelia turned to speak to Maggie. "Just tell me one thing," she said. "What was the name of the girl with the golden goose?"

"I don't know. She never told me," said Maggie. She hated lying, but there was no way she was going to tell Zelia that the girl's name was Stella.

"Then at least tell me what she looked like," Zelia said.

Maggie shook her head. "Not in a hundred years!"

Zelia scowled and was about to say something, but Bob was already closing the door.

"That explains why Zelia wanted me back," said Maggie once the door was shut. "She wanted me to find the girl with the goose."

"I'm sure you're right," said Bob.

"Thank you both for letting me stay with you!" Maggie cried, throwing her arms around Bob and Nora. "When the fish said he'd grant my wish, I was going to wish for a nicer family, but he started swimming away before I could tell him."

"So you never made your wish?" asked Nora.

Maggie shrugged. "He was leaving when I said it. I didn't say it very loudly because I didn't want

Peter to hear me, so I wasn't sure the fish heard me either. But I think he must have, because my wish really did come true. I couldn't have found a nicer family than you and Bob!"

Chapter 12

After Maggie and Bob had finished eating their breakfast, they went to the stable to feed the magical animals. Maggie was giving grain to the old, white unicorn when she heard someone call, "Hello! Is anyone here?"

Shutting the stall door behind her, Maggie hurried to see who was there. It was Stella, holding her goose, Eglantine.

Bob finished scooping grain into buckets and turned around. "Who is it?" he asked, joining Maggie at the door.

"Stella and Eglantine," said Maggie. "Stella is the girl. Eglantine is her goose."

"Are you the man who helps magic animals?" Stella asked him.

"I am," said Bob. "Is something wrong with your goose?"

Stella nodded. "She hurt her foot, but she won't let me look at it."

"Ah!" said Bob. "Let me see what I can do."

At first the goose wouldn't let him touch her

webbed foot, but when he used a soft voice and gentle hands, she finally let him hold it. "She has a tiny thorn in her foot," Bob said.

"Can you take the thorn out?" asked Stella.

"Of course," Bob replied. A moment later he had the thorn in his hand and was showing it to Stella. "I have some ointment you can put on Eglantine's foot, but it might be sore for a day or two. Stay here and I'll get the ointment."

When Bob hurried off, Stella turned to Maggie. "I can't believe Eglantine held still for him like that!"

Maggie smiled. "Bob has a way with magical animals."

"Do you live here, too?" Stella asked her.

"I do now," said Maggie.

"If you two are just going to stand around gabbing, would one of you mind brushing my back? I have an itchy spot I can't reach," said Leonard.

Stella looked startled. "Did that horse just talk?" she whispered to Maggie.

"That's Leonard," said Maggie. "He's a talking horse."

Leonard snorted. "What did she think I was, a talking butterfly? So, are you going to brush me or not?"

"You should be happy that I fed you first today," said Maggie. "I'll brush you after I finish feeding everyone else."

"This place is wonderful!" exclaimed Stella. "I have to take

Eglantine home as soon as I get the ointment from Bob, but do you think he would mind if I came back someday?"

"I don't think he'd mind at all," Maggie told her. "Maybe you can help me teach the piglets how to fly."

"I'd love that!" said Stella. "You're lucky you get to live in such a wonderful place!"

"I know!" said Maggie. "And it's all because of a fish!"

About the Author

E. D. Baker is the author of the Tales of the Frog Princess series, the Wide-Awake Princess series, the Fairy-Tale Matchmaker series, and many other delightful books for young readers, including *A Question of Magic*,

Fairy Wings, and *Fairy Lies*. Her first book, *The Frog Princess*, was the inspiration for Disney's hit movie *The Princess and the Frog*. She lives with her family and their many animals in rural Maryland.

www.talesofedbaker.com